VENGEANCE OF THE PINK FLAMINGO

"I'M PINK THEREFORE I AM"

◆ FriesenPress

Suite 300 - 990 Fort St
Victoria, BC, V8V 3K2
Canada

www.friesenpress.com

Copyright © 2018 by G. R. Hurlburt
First Edition — 2018

All rights reserved.

No part of this publication may be reproduced in any form, or by any means, electronic or mechanical, including photocopying, recording, or any information browsing, storage, or retrieval system, without permission in writing from FriesenPress.

ISBN
978-1-5255-2947-4 (Hardcover)
978-1-4602-9050-7 (Paperback)
978-1-4602-9051-4 (eBook)

1. FIC052000 FICTION SATIRE

Distributed to the trade by The Ingram Book Company
Available for sale at https://books.friesenpress.com/store

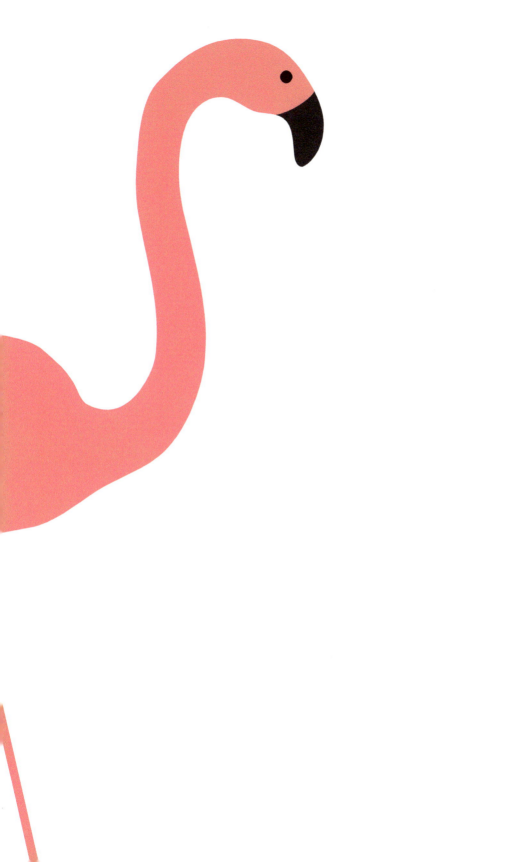

In 3007, archaeologists excavating a pre-war town in eastern North America uncover a plaster pink flamingo surrounded by grave goods. Such idols stood in sacred clearings called "lawns" in the twenty-first century, apparently to propitiate the powerful household god "Tah-Kee-Niss".

VENGEANCE OF THE PINK FLAMINGO 2

The excited archaeologists set the flamingo up inside an enclosure, in mockery of ancient customs, and drive off to drink beer.

VENGEANCE OF THE PINK FLAMINGO 4

However, unknown to the archaeologists, radiation has induced mutations in the DNA of the tiny organisms whose calcareous skeletons compose the lime in the flamingo's plaster. Eerily he comes to life and breaks out of the enclosure to search for others of his kind.

VENGEANCE OF THE PINK FLAMINGO 6

But he finds only destruction, and the unmistakable mark of man. The few birds to survive the war were persecuted by the desperate populace, mistaking them for aircraft.

VENGEANCE OF THE PINK FLAMINGO

The enraged avian breaks into a mansion, vowing vengeance on the inhabitants.

VENGEANCE OF THE PINK FLAMINGO 10

The berserk lawn ornament rampages through the house, breaking down doors and smashing walls in a search for victims.

VENGEANCE OF THE PINK FLAMINGO 12

But he finds no prey. The next morning, townsfolk investigating the night's commotion find him lying in a drunken stupor and wearing no pants.

VENGEANCE OF THE PINK FLAMINGO 14

He is rushed to court, found guilty of indecent exposure and public intoxication, and jailed for a year.

VENGEANCE OF THE PINK FLAMINGO 16

While imprisoned, he examines his life and concludes he must learn to adjust.

VENGEANCE OF THE PINK FLAMINGO 18

Resolved to make the best of his incarceration, he takes advantage of the prison training system and learns a trade.

VENGEANCE OF THE PINK FLAMINGO

He finds employment when his time is up. However, the size of his hat and other working conditions are not agreeable and he finds himself yearning for meaning.

VENGEANCE OF THE PINK FLAMINGO

A photojournalist takes an interest in his story. A brief love affair fizzles, but he finds the courage to quit his job and find more fulfilling employment.

VENGEANCE OF THE PINK FLAMINGO 24

He is hired by a tree with a travelling circus and given second billing to a trio of nude dwarf acrobats.

VENGEANCE OF THE PINK FLAMINGO 26

After several years of steady growth, the tree attempts to branch out the circus operations. The result is collapse, financially for the circus and physically for the tree. Taking the tide in the affairs of men at its flood, the flamingo uses his savings to buy out the tree.

He becomes a Muslim and marries all his female staff. All employees of an appropriate age are adopted; the rest are terminated on religious grounds. The ensuing tax advantages ensure financial success for the circus. He has plastic surgery to change his appearance and is left feeling hollow.

VENGEANCE OF THE PINK FLAMINGO 30

At age sixty, he changes his prosperous, settled life. In an imposing government building, he fills out forms in quadruplicate, annoys secretaries by interrupting their conversations, and is repeatedly sent from the right floor three floors up to the wrong floor. Finally, he bribes a judge and in fifteen minutes succeeds in selling the circus, divorcing his wives with fat settlements, and disinheriting all children who will not become lawyers, doctors, or accountants.

VENGEANCE OF THE PINK FLAMINGO 32

With a few dollars in his pockets, he sets off to see the world. Travelling widely, he encounters many strange cultures, some too poor to afford colour. Resting in Nepal, he determines to journey to the Himalayas.

VENGEANCE OF THE PINK FLAMINGO 34

The flamingo wanders deep into the mountains and discovers a remote plateau surrounded by deep valleys. Crossing a bridge of ice and snow, he climbs the plateau side, coming upon an unknown monastery with marvelous lawns.

VENGEANCE OF THE PINK FLAMINGO 36

He is welcomed into the monastery and becomes a Buddhist, rising among the monks through his administrative abilities. He establishes his own lawnasery, and devotes his life to comprehending the essence of being through proper lawn maintenance.

VENGEANCE OF THE PINK FLAMINGO 38

But tranquility is not so easily had. Wandering late one evening in contemplation, he discovers an invasion force, a renegade column of communist Chinese meaning to replace the repressive Tibetan feudal system with a repressive modern totalitarian system.

VENGEANCE OF THE PINK FLAMINGO 40

With the first rays of dawn, the flamingo watches from a high cliff as the invaders advance across the ice bridge. He voices the first harsh, piercing notes of the death song of the pink flamingo. The discordant, screeching sounds shatter the ice of the bridge and bring avalanches down from the surrounding mountainsides.

VENGEANCE OF THE PINK FLAMINGO 42

As the ice bridge collapses, rocks crumble and collapse under the flamingo's feet, and he is carried down with the rock slides. At the bottom of the unbridgeable chasm lie buried the red Chinese and the pink flamingo, with only his legs exposed.

Is this the end for the flamingo, or just inadvertent cryogenic freezing?

VENGEANCE OF THE PINK FLAMINGO 44

45   GRANT HURLBURT

ACKNOWLEDGEMENTS

For comments, editing expertise, encouragement, patience, invaluable help with Photoshop (P), and for laughing before asking whether the book was meant to be funny: Mollie Ashley (P); Greg Arnett; Madeleine Arnett; Shannon Blanke; Anita Bernstein; Naomi Bernstein; Bryanna Blackwell (P); Rufus Churcher; Carolyn Cote; Astra Crompton; Rick Cook; Steve Cooper; Janet Cooper; Ian Craine; Peter Dolan; Leigh Dayton; Sylvia Dayton; Mike Dennison; Dena Doroschenko; FriesenPress; Leia Gehr; Hank Heather; Sharilyn Ingram; Adrian Jaspan (P); Nicholas Jaspan; Andy Kaufman; Vince Klemen; Ed Knapp; Olga Kovolsky; Daniel Kozlovic; Margaret Kozerawski; Dennis Lee; Franki Marcussen; Dale Mark; Ian Morrison; Pegi O'Grady; Kay Pearson; David Rudkin; Terry Ryan; Jean Perry; Elaine Rousseau; Carolyn Smith; Ashley Starbucks; Patrick Starbucks (P); and various anonymous Starbucks customers and Indigo staff.

Apologies to anyone I've missed.

47 GRANT HURLBURT

"I'M PINK THEREFORE I AM"

Also Available
SON OF THE PINK FLAMINGO

Both *Son of Pink Flamingo* and *Vengeance of the Pink Flamingo* are available for sale at FriesenPress.com

49   GRANT HURLBURT

Author with Peregrine Falcon ("sheheen" in Arabic). Flamingos just don't perch well.